# BENJAMIN'S NEW BEGINNING

*Amish Romance*

## HANNAH MILLER

Tica House
Publishing

Sweet Romance that Delights and Enchants!

# Personal Word from the Author

**To My Dear Readers,**

How exciting that you have chosen one of my books to read. Thank you! I am proud to now be part of the team of writers at Tica House Publishing who work joyfully to bring you stories of hope, faith, courage, and love.

Please feel free to contact me as I love to hear from my readers. I would like to personally invite you to sign up for updates and to become part of our **Exclusive Reader Club** —it's completely Free to join! Hope to see you there!

**With love,**

**Hannah Miller**

## VISIT HERE to Join our Reader's Club and to Receive Tica House Updates:

https://amish.subscribemenow.com/

# Chapter One

Evelyn Lantz flinched as she heard the voice of her stepmother call for her. Her *new* stepmother, for Greta had married Evelyn's widowed father only six months ago. At first, Evelyn was happy for her *daed* and had welcomed Greta into the family. But now Evelyn had become a bit impatient with Greta.

Evelyn blew out her breath in frustration. It didn't seem she could get anything done without Greta constantly interrupting her. Greta was only a few months older than Evelyn, but it seemed she was much more immature. She didn't like to work and was used to being waited on. Since Evelyn was the only daughter and the youngest of four siblings, she was the one at Greta's beck and call. Her three older brothers were married and had homes of their own.

Even if they weren't married and gone, Evelyn knew they wouldn't have waited on Greta.

Evelyn gave the dust mop another swipe across the floor before she answered her stepmother. She wondered for the hundredth time why Greta, only twenty-three, had married Evelyn's forty-nine-year-old father. Maybe she was trying to replace her own father who had died the year before. Or maybe she just fancied older men. Evelyn wasn't sure the reason, but she wished whatever the attraction was, it hadn't been strong enough to lure her father into the marriage.

Now that Greta was expecting a *boppli*, things were worse than ever. She'd suffered some morning sickness early on and used that as an excuse to lie around and act even more helpless.

Evelyn strode into the bedroom where Greta, still in her nightgown, lounged on the bed. "What do you need, Greta?"

"I'm dying of thirst, Evelyn. Would you be sweet and bring me a glass of water?"

Evelyn nodded and left the room, trying not to feel resentful. She knew it wasn't a very Christian-like attitude, but she couldn't help but feel angry at Greta. Greta was young and healthy. There was no reason she couldn't have gotten off that bed and gotten her own drink of water. She hadn't thrown up this morning as she hadn't been nauseous, so why couldn't she move her feet? Millions of women worked their way through pregnancy.

Evelyn knew, of course, there were exceptions, but she didn't believe Greta was one of them. She seemed fine that morning, she had good color, and she didn't appear weak. So why the helpless act?

*Because she's lazy.* Evelyn shocked herself with the thought. When had she grown so bitter? It wasn't like her to be judgmental. She was normally a compassionate, caring person, not a malicious and vindictive.

She got a glass of water and carried it back to Greta, who was now surrounded by scattered books and snacks. For a moment, she fought an urge to set the water glass across the room so Greta would have to get up to retrieve it.

*Ach*, goodness, this had gone too far. Evelyn was alarming herself with such thoughts.

"Here's your water, Greta. I'm about to start lunch. Is there anything special you want?" She made the offer in an attempt to atone for her mean thoughts.

"I am feeling hungry. And I'm better now, so I think I'll get up and get dressed and come to the table for lunch." Greta swung her legs over the edge of the bed. "How about a grilled cheese sandwich and some tomato soup?"

Evelyn nodded and retreated to the kitchen. At least, Greta wasn't expecting this meal brought to her in bed on a tray like sh'd demanded that morning. Evelyn pulled the cast iron skillet from the cabinet and got out the bread and butter. She made herself repeat Bible verses about patience while she cooked the sandwiches and heated the soup she had canned last summer.

She carried the food into the dining room where Greta waited. Why she sat there instead of at the kitchen table, Evelyn didn't know. She guessed it made her feel more like the lady of the house with servants waiting on her.

*Stop it*, she scolded herself. *You are being terrible.*

"Aren't you going to eat with me?" Greta asked, turning blue eyes toward Evelyn. "I've been pretty lonely lately. Your father is so busy with work. I am proud because he is a much sought-after carpenter, but it seems he's never home."

"I'll bring my food in," Evelyn said, instead of following her instinct to snap at Greta that *Daed* had to work to make money to take care of his new wife and the coming baby.

She ran her hand over her eyes, fighting against a headache, then grabbed her plate and bowl and carried them into the dining room. She sat down and bowed her head in silent prayer, praying once again for patience and tolerance.

When the meal was nearly finished, Greta wiped her mouth with a napkin and said, "That was a good lunch, Evelyn, but I've had the strongest craving for bananas. I don't think I can stand to go another day without one. Were you planning on going to town today?"

"I hadn't really planned on it. The weather's a little nasty, and I was going to start making myself a new dress for preaching service."

"Hmm. I guess I'll have to go myself. I just hope the buggy ride doesn't make me sick like it did the other week."

Evelyn winced. Greta had thrown up on the ride to church two weeks before. Guilt washed over her, and she gave in.

"*Nee, nee,* I'll go," she said. "My dress can wait."

"Thank you, Evelyn. I do appreciate it."

"I'll just wash these few dishes and go hitch Maggie." She gathered up the plates and bowls and took them to the kitchen. She then glanced around to see if there was anything else they needed since she was going to the grocery.

The trip to town was rather miserable. It was the middle of January, and the wind was blowing mightily. The rain came steadily down, cold and wet. By the time she made it to the store and got everything she needed, loaded it all into the buggy, and drove back again, she was soaked and chilly.

However, on the way, she focused on calming herself, blanking out the niggling pain behind her eyes. She prayed, as she often did, as if she were having an intimate conversation with *Gott.* It made her feel less stressed, more at peace, and gave her strength enough to deal with Greta again.

Her heart skipped a beat when she pulled into the drive and saw Mark King's horse and buggy tied to the hitching post. Mark had been courting her lately. She was quite smitten with him, too, even though he was a bit gruff around the edges and not the most handsome bachelor in the district.

She thought he was nice, though, and she had to admit she wasn't getting any younger. She might not have many more chances to marry a good man like Mark. Even if she didn't feel the kind of thrill she yearned to experience when she was near her future husband, he was definitely a good man.

She wondered what he was doing here now. She didn't think they had plans to meet this afternoon. She racked her brain but couldn't think of anything she'd forgotten. Maybe he had just wanted to surprise her, she thought. She rather liked the idea. But now, she could sneak quietly into the house and surprise him instead.

She drove to the barn and unhitched Maggie then gave her a good feeding before she headed into the house. She slipped in quietly and tiptoed over to the door between the kitchen and the dining room where she could hear the rumble of their voices.

"Honestly, Mark, I don't know why she says she doesn't want to marry you," Greta said. "Any woman with any sense would want to. After all, you have a thriving farm, you're strong, and a good Christian man. She certainly couldn't do better than you, but she's bullheaded, you know. I just don't want you to waste your time and end up with a broken heart."

# Chapter Two

Shock sizzled through Evelyn. She had never said she didn't want to marry Mark. Why was Greta blatantly lying to him? Confusion washed over her. She couldn't think of one reason Greta would be going on so. Or maybe she did.

Did Greta want to ruin Evelyn's prospects for marriage so she would be forced to stay here and be a servant to her stepmother?

Surely, Mark wouldn't believe Greta. He knew her better than that. At least, she hoped he did. She wondered how he would react to Greta's lies. Would he act any differently to her? Would he ask her about it? The truth was, he hadn't yet proposed to her. He might not say one word to her about Greta's words for that reason alone.

As quietly as she could, Evelyn slipped back across the kitchen floor and slammed the door as if she were just coming in. She plopped the bags she carried on the table and called out.

"I'm home, Greta. Is that Mark's buggy I saw out front?"

"Oh, you're home. *Jah*, Mark is in here. Come in and say hello," came Greta's reply.

Greta walked into the dining room where Mark and Greta sat at the table, plates scattered with crumbs from the apple pie Evelyn had made that morning. Mark looked a bit sheepish, but Greta was as cool as ever.

"I'm afraid I told Mark I didn't know where you were. I forgot you said you were going to the store," Greta informed her.

How could she have forgotten? Evelyn wondered. She'd only gone because Greta wanted her to. Was Greta deliberately sabotaging her? Suspicion grew inside her.

"I got the bananas you asked for," Evelyn clearly stated.

"*Denki*. Now, if you'll excuse me, I think I'll go lie down for a while. It was good to see you, Mark."

Evelyn stared at Greta's departing back. She was irritated with the woman. For some reason, Greta seemed to be trying to disrupt Evelyn's relationship with Mark.

"That woman can be downright hateful sometimes," she muttered.

"What was that?" Mark asked.

She hadn't realized he'd moved closer to her, and she turned to face him.

"Nothing ... nothing at all," she said but she saw him raise his eyebrows doubtfully. "Umm. It's just that ... well, Greta and I haven't been getting along very well."

"Why not? She seems sweet to me."

Evelyn couldn't help it. She snorted softly. "Perhaps... However, she did know where I was. She knew perfectly well. I only went to the store because she asked me to."

"That sounds a bit harsh, Evelyn. Maybe you're just being impatient with her."

"Impatient?" Evelyn took a slow breath, not wanting to get into this too deeply. Yet, she felt compelled to defend herself. "I've been doing my best to be helpful to her. I went to town to get her bananas, of all things. She knew exactly where I was."

"Maybe she is still adjusting to life in this house and being married to your father. Her own father has only been gone for a year." Mark's voice was full of sympathy.

Evelyn's frayed nerves snapped. "That doesn't make it all right for her to take advantage of me, Mark. It's gotten to be too much."

Mark was clearly shocked that she had spoken so sharply. She had never raised her voice to him before. She knew it was not Christ-like, but she couldn't help it. She'd taken too much for too long.

She shouldn't take her frustration out on Mark, though. She drew in a deep breath and apologized.

"I'm sorry," she said. "I shouldn't have snapped at you."

He considered her words for a moment, and then said, "I'm sorry, too. I know things can get tense between family members sometimes."

Evelyn felt this was oversimplifying things, but she now regretted her outburst, so she said nothing.

"I just stopped by to say hello for a moment. I'm on my way to the farrier to set up an appointment for our horses. I should be going."

"I'm sorry I wasn't here when you came," she said, wishing the entire meeting hadn't happened at all. What must he think of her?

"I'll see you soon, Evelyn."

"*Jah*. I'll see you soon."

Evelyn watched him leave with mixed feelings. She had to wonder about their relationship. She wished there was more fun between them, more lightness. She wished they laughed together more—which was both of their faults, she supposed. She did want a husband and a home of her own. She wanted *kinner*. But she was beginning to doubt Mark King was the man for her.

Something didn't feel right about their relationship and today had only highlighted that fact. Did she really want to spend the rest of her life with him? She simply wasn't sure anymore.

What she was sure of was she needed a break from Greta and her demanding ways. Maybe she would talk to each of her brothers and see if she could stay with one of them for a while.

Her brothers all lived within fifty miles. She wouldn't be too far away if she were needed home in a hurry for some reason, but she'd be far enough away to avoid impulse visits. They say absence makes the heart grow fonder. Maybe she could put that adage to the test.

With that thought in mind, she sat down that evening and wrote a letter to each of her brothers.

# Chapter Three

Evelyn peered out the window of the van that was taking her to her brother Dan's house. She had finally heard back from him and was relieved when he said he and his wife would be happy to have her. She could help take care of her niece and nephew as Rachel was nearing the due date of the birth of their third child.

She hired a driver to take her to Dan's, and they were nearing their destination now. It was a cold, sunny day and Evelyn enjoyed taking in the pastoral scenery. The lustrous blue sky shimmered above, ribbons of lacy white clouds rippling across it. Blowing bare branches danced in many of the yards they passed. She had the window cracked open so she could enjoy the smell of the fresh, cool air.

Finally, the driver pulled into the driveway of a big, white house and Evelyn hopped out and waved as Rachel came out on the porch. Her sister-in-law was one of Evelyn's favorite people in the world, and she squealed with delight as she ran to the porch to greet her with a big hug.

"It's so *gut* to see you, Evelyn," Rachel said. "*Kinner*, say hello to your *Aenti* Evelyn."

Five-year-old Teddy stepped up and greeted her confidently, but four-year-old Mary was a bit shy and hid behind her brother. All Evelyn could see was her blonde curls and big blue eyes poking out from behind his back.

"Hello, Mary. Remember me? We played together at Christmas." She spoke softly and grinned at the little girl. "You beat me at pin the tail on the donkey, remember?"

A bright smile crossed the little girl's face and though she nodded happily, she still didn't speak. Evelyn remembered Mary had been one of the quietest children at the family holiday gathering.

"Dan should be in for lunch in a little bit. He's glad you're staying with us for a while. Oh, and you're not the only guest we're having. My cousin Benjamin Glick is here, too. He's staying in a room we fixed up over the barn."

This was news to Evelyn. "I hope I'm not one person too many for you," she said worriedly.

"Of course not, especially if you're willing to help tend the *kinner*. It's getting a little hard for me to keep up with them." Rachel grinned and rubbed her protruding belly.

"You know I'll be happy to help out. I want to be useful."

The women and children moved inside, Evelyn carrying her suitcase.

"Your room is upstairs, the first room on the left. Mary's room is right across from you, and Teddy's is next door. Dan and I have the room next to that."

"I remember. I'll go up and unpack and be right back down," Evelyn said and started up the stairs to her room. It was fairly small but sufficient. She quickly hung up her dresses on the pegs and put away the rest of her things. There. That was done.

Evelyn checked her hair, tucking a few stray strands beneath her *kapp*, then headed down the stairs. A sense of relief washed over her as she descended. Being away from Greta was going to make life much easier for her. Admittedly, her father wasn't happy with her for choosing to go to Dan's, but hopefully, he would adjust to the idea. Besides, she wouldn't be gone forever.

She rounded the corner as she came down the stairs and stopped abruptly to behold a large man standing in the foyer. Rachel and the *kinner* were nowhere in sight.

"Hello."

The man turned around to look at her. He was tall, very tall, Evelyn realized. His hair was almost black, and his eyes were an amazing shade of ice blue fringed with long, dark lashes. She had to fight an urge to touch the cleft in his chin.

Dimples flashed as he grinned. "You must be Dan's sister. I'm Rachel's cousin, Benjamin."

Of course, he was. But Rachel hadn't warned her he was a good-looking giant, however. The sheer size of him made Evelyn feel a bit intimidated.

"Hello. It's nice to meet you," she said. "Were you looking for something?"

"*Jah*. I'm looking for lunch. I brought in the mail, too." He held up the envelopes he'd been about to toss on the dining table.

"Well, maybe Rachel is in the kitchen. Should we go see?"

Benjamin nodded, and they walked toward the back of the house. Rachel was there at the stove and the *kinner* were seated at the table, each with a banana in hand.

"Hello. I see you two met," Rachel said as she flipped hamburger patties in a frying pan. "Oh, and here's Dan."

Dan Lantz came in and gave Evelyn a big hug.

"Hi, Evelyn. You look happy and well."

"I am, especially since I'm here." She felt a load of stress off her shoulders already. It wasn't that she minded doing the work at home. She'd been doing it all for years anyway—ever since her mother had died when she was twelve. What she minded was Greta pretending she was incapable of helping and not contributing anything to the household. Surely, things would be better here.

"How can I help, Rachel?" Evelyn asked.

"You can get the ketchup and mustard out of the fridge," Rachel answered, and Evelyn moved to do as she asked.

"So, Ben, did you get the goats moved to the other pasture?" Dan asked.

"I did. They were cavorting and playing like a pack of kittens," Ben said. "How did the meeting with Joe Linzer go?"

"Right *gut*. I think we have a new customer for our goats' milk." Soon they were all sitting at the table. They took a moment for silent prayer before starting on the burgers and fries Rachel had prepared.

Ben looked at Evelyn and said, "It's a nice place here. I find myself glad I was banished here by my mother because I was seeing an *Englisch* woman. What is your story?"

Evelyn almost spit out the sip of tea she had just taken. She couldn't believe how forward he was being.

"I-I..." She swallowed. "I wasn't banished. I chose to be here."

He gave a hearty laugh. "*Gut* to know."

"So... when is your banishment over?" she asked, daring to tease him a bit.

"Ha! Not sure. I like it here, very much. More than I thought I would. In fact, I'm thinking about staying in the area. Dan here has taught me a lot about goat farming. I might go into it myself."

She took another sip of tea, trying not to stare at him. He was unlike anyone she'd ever met. And she was still shocked by his boldness. She shook her head and took a bite of her sandwich. She had a feeling life with Benjamin was going to be interesting.

# Chapter Four

Evelyn peered out the window early the next morning. The sun had barely begun to climb over the horizon, but it seemed to promise to be another beautiful winter day. She decided not to waste time and hurried to get dressed and go downstairs.

Despite the early hour, Rachel was already in the kitchen. She smiled and greeted Evelyn, pouring them each a cup of *kaffee* before asking, "How did you sleep?"

"I slept well, *denki*," Evelyn answered. "What can I do to help?"

"Would you mind collecting the eggs and feeding the chickens?"

"Of course not. I'll just get my coat and go do that."

The air was cool when she stepped outside, and she pulled her coat closer. There wasn't any wind, though, and stillness reigned supreme. Evelyn took a moment to say a prayer thanking *Gott* for giving her the chance to come and enjoy her brother's family.

The chicken coop was located down the hill next to the barn. She strolled along, relishing the shadows of dawn and the sweet smell of the fresh air.

She pulled open the door of the hen house and lit the lamp by the door. Most of the chickens clucked softly and hopped off their roosts and strutted toward the open door. A few still squatted blearily on their nests, not yet ready to start their day.

"Hello, chickies," she said and moved to collect the eggs. One or two of the hens didn't like her taking their treasures but she was quick and managed to avoid the pecks. When she was finished, she turned and headed out the door.

"Boo!"

The deep voice coming out of nowhere made Evelyn jump and the egg basket flew out of her hand. Evelyn groaned as two of the eggs fell and broke on her shoes. She whirled and glared at Benjamin who was approaching from the direction of the barn.

"Look what you've done," she cried. "I broke the eggs, and my shoes are a mess."

"*Ach,* I'm sorry, Evelyn. I didn't mean to scare you. Let me help you clean up." He bent to remove the shells from her shoes.

"Do you always go around scaring people?" she couldn't help but ask.

"Nope. Just you, it seems."

She stared at him. She simply didn't know what to make of him.

"Don't be mad. I'll make it up to you."

"I-I'm not mad."

He raised a brow at that. "Well, I am sorry I made you drop the eggs. Come on, I'll confess what happened to Rachel."

Evelyn drew in a deep breath to steady herself. "That's not necessary. I can tell her what happened."

"*Nee,* I'm going to take the blame. I wouldn't want you to experience anything bad over something I did."

"Rachel's not like that," Evelyn protested. "She's very sweet. She'll understand it was all your fault."

"Ha! But then, I'm not the one who tossed the basket in the air," he said, with a twinkle in his eyes.

"*Nee,* you're just the one who caused me to send it flying."

She heard him chuckle as she walked in front of him toward the house.

"Wait, Evelyn," he said, and she turned.

"What is it now?"

"I just wanted to tell you how pretty you are when you're angry."

Her mouth fell open, and she stared at him. "You are ... you are the most exasperating man I have ever met."

"*Denki.* I try my best."

Speechless, she groaned and whipped around to continue into the house.

Rachel smiled as they both came into the kitchen. "Did you get the eggs?"

"Well..." Evelyn started.

"Evelyn dropped the eggs and broke them," Benjamin said quickly. "Got them all over her shoes, too."

Evelyn sputtered and whirled to face him once again. She had to tip her head back to glare into his face and was astonished to see his lips twitching and the dimples dancing in his cheeks.

"Rachel, your cousin is terrible," she cried. "That is not what happened at all."

"She's right, Rachel. I was coming up from the barn and saw her coming out of the henhouse. I couldn't resist and shouted *boo* at her, and she jumped a mile. The basket went flying and so did the eggs. I'm sorry."

"Why didn't you say that in the first place?" Evelyn sputtered.

"Because I love to see your cheeks get pink and your eyes flash when you're aggravated. You don't have that red hair for nothing, do you?" he said and winked at her. "Now, I need to get back out and help Dan with the milking. We'll be back in about half an hour."

Evelyn stared at his departing back and blew out a long, exasperated breath. The man was as full of brass as one of those *Englisch* marching bands.

She heard Rachel giggle and turned to look at her.

"I'm sorry, but Benjamin always makes me laugh. I love having him here."

"He's ... he's—" Evelyn was at a loss for words.

"He'll grow on you, I'm sure."

"That will be interesting," Evelyn muttered.

"Just give him a chance," Rachel said softly. "I would appreciate it."

Evelyn nodded and drew in a deep shuddering breath. She didn't know if she and Benjamin could possibly get along, but she supposed it would be a favor to Rachel. She was willing to try. The rest would be up to him.

"Besides," Rachel said, a twinkle in her hazel eyes. "I think he likes you."

Color flamed in Evelyn's cheeks. Rachel was sadly mistaken, of course.

"If he liked me, why would he act so brash and unpleasant? I don't think so."

"Well, it's just a feeling I have. A look I see on his face when he looks at you or something..."

"That's the look of him plotting what he can do to annoy me next," Evelyn said with a soft snort.

"Even if it is, that means you're on his mind," Rachel said as she flipped a pancake. "It's time to get the *kinner* up. Would you mind doing that for me, please?"

Evelyn nodded and left the room, but she was still thinking about what Rachel had said about Benjamin liking her. Was he acting like a little boy with a crush on a girl, trying to win her attention by chasing her with snakes or eating a worm in front of her?

The thought made her smile. Acting like a little boy was exactly what she would expect of Benjamin Glick.

# Chapter Five

Evelyn spent the next couple of days settling in at Dan's place. She felt a sense of relief being out of Greta's grasp and enjoyed the atmosphere here. Rachel and Dan seemed happy, and the *kinner* were content and well-mannered. The farm was beautiful, and she enjoyed being on the bank of the river that was lined with magnificent weeping willow trees, despite the cold weather.

The only thorn, so to speak, was Benjamin. Fortunately, she'd been able to avoid him most of the time and only had to deal with him at meals. She did feel his gaze on her frequently at mealtimes, and she found herself squirming in her chair at times. Why was he always looking at her, anyway?

Evelyn had familiarized herself with the farm and the routine but had yet to go into the nearby town. She was hoping

Rachel would be able to accompany her there this afternoon. Evelyn wanted to visit the library and perhaps use Rachel's library card, and she also hoped to visit the grocery store and get some of the ingredients she needed to make her favorite baked goods. She particularly wanted to make some of her special brownies as a treat for the family.

She and Rachel were working together after breakfast to *red* up the kitchen when she brought the subject up.

"Oh, Evelyn, I would love to, but I told Norma Lapp I would come by and stay with her *kinner* this afternoon while she goes to the doctor. My two are going with me, so you'll be free. Why don't I ask Benjamin if he could take you?"

"Oh, *nee*, that's not necessary," Evelyn hurried to answer. "I don't want to bother Benjamin. Besides, you'll need the buggy."

"Don't want to bother me about what?" Benjamin's voice suddenly came from behind her, and Evelyn spun to face him.

"Evelyn was saying she'd like to get more acquainted with the town." Rachel wiped the tabletop as she spoke. "I suggested you might take her."

"I'd be happy to do that. I have to go to town today anyway and pick up some lumber. We can take the wagon." He pushed his hat back on his head and grinned as he made the offer.

"*Nee*, really, it's not necessary," Evelyn objected. "I don't need to go."

"Don't be silly. I'm going anyway, and there's room on the wagon seat for one more."

"I don't want to hold you up." Evelyn waved her hand in protest.

"I got a tour when I came a few weeks ago, now it's my turn to give you the tour."

"Go on, Evelyn," Rachel urged. "It will be *gut* for you to get out for a while. And there's not much bite to the air today."

Evelyn couldn't think of any more excuses, so she finally nodded reluctantly.

"*Gut.* We'll go right after lunch if that suits you."

"I'll be ready."

Evelyn spent the time until they were ready to go dreading the hours ahead. She didn't want to be alone with Benjamin. He asked too many questions. He didn't think enough before he spoke. She just didn't feel comfortable with him—even if he did have lovely blue eyes and thick muscles beneath his flannel shirt.

She finished wiping off the cabinet tops then ran upstairs to check her hair and grab her shawl. She took a deep breath and prayed for grace before she headed out to the buggy. *Please,*

*Lord, I don't want to fight with Benjamin today. Let this time be pleasant.*

He was waiting with the wagon and grinned when she appeared, saying, "Let's go have an adventure."

"I don't know about that," Evelyn replied as she climbed up onto the seat. "Just a nice, calm trip into town will do, *denki*."

"Okay, nice and calm it is," he said, then flipped the reins and set the horse off at a brisk trot. Evelyn grabbed the seat and hung on, gritting her teeth and ordering herself to keep her mouth shut. He was just trying to get a rise out of her.

Benjamin slowed the wagon as he turned onto the road and held it down to an even trot. Evelyn let her breath out and felt some of the tension leave her shoulders. She relaxed and allowed herself to enjoy the scenery.

The clopping of the horse's hooves made a rhythmic sound she found soothing, and the temperature became warm for January. If she could just forget whom she was with, she could enjoy this trip into town. She leaned back and closed her eyes, enjoying the sun playing across her face. A gentle breeze tickled her skin, and she could hear the sounds of the river gurgling nearby. Peace and tranquility washed over her, and she gave herself permission to indulge in the feelings.

"Look, Evelyn," Benjamin suddenly hissed, "a doe and a buck."

Evelyn opened her eyes and followed his pointing finger. The two deer gazed at them with perked ears. They were on the other side of the river and had been drinking from the icy water.

"It's like a picture postcard," Evelyn whispered. "Beautiful."

"I hated to wake you, but I thought you'd want to see that," Ben said with a grin.

"I wasn't asleep. I was just...resting my eyes." She blushed as she spoke. "And enjoying the unseasonable weather."

"It is a glorious day," he said. "The Lord has been *gut* to us today."

"He's *gut* to us every day," Evelyn reminded him.

"*Jah*, you're right." Benjamin nodded and rubbed his hand across his chin. "I need to remind myself of that more often."

His words surprised her. "Oh?"

"It's just some things that have happened in my life the last year or two. I meant it's important for me to keep the *gut* things in life at the forefront of my mind."

She didn't push, but her curiosity was ignited. She let him distract her when he pointed out the covered bridge that led into town and the wooden sign next to it.

"Welcome to Shiloh Creek," she read. "Population six thousand and six."

"*Jah*. It's not a big place, but I like it here. I think you might, too. Look, here's the park."

Evelyn glanced over to the river, where a small waterfall was rushing over its apex. Weeping willows draped over the banks and geese paddled on the surface of the water. Bundled up toddlers enjoyed themselves on the nearby playground, with parents keeping a watchful eye from surrounding benches.

"It's a sweet little park," Evelyn commented.

"Dan told me they have festivals there about three times a year. In fact, the winter festival is going to be next week. Maybe we can go together that day."

His words took Evelyn by surprise. She was unsure how to respond.

"I-I don't know, Benjamin. We might come as a family," she finally said.

"*Jah*, you're right. Maybe the whole family will come. That would be fun. I'd enjoy watching Teddy and Mary."

She sighed with relief at his easy acceptance of her response. Coming to the festival with him alone would seem too much like a date.

"I've got to go to the lumberyard. Where did you want to go?" he asked.

"I'd like to go to the library."

"Okay. How about I drop you off there and come back in about half an hour or so?"

"Sounds *gut*."

He pulled up in front of a brick building and Evelyn climbed out. She walked into the library and looked around, surprised by how large the interior was. She floated around looking at the many books. She loved libraries, and this one was surprisingly extensive. She poured over books from around the world, letting herself get lost in the pictures of mountains and oceans.

She selected a couple of books to take home with her and carried them to the checkout counter. A smiling young *Englisch* woman looked up and greeted her.

"Hi. I'd like to use my sister's library card to check these books out."

The woman glanced around and then said in a conspiratorial voice, "We don't usually allow that, but I think I can make an exception."

Evelyn was tugging her sister-in-law's card from her purse when the librarian gasped breathlessly.

"Ben."

# Chapter Six

Evelyn turned and saw a grinning Benjamin behind her.

"Hello, Penny. I see you're helping my cousin's sister-in-law."

Penny's cheeks pinkened, and she batted her eyelashes behind tortoiseshell glasses. "Yes, she's checking out some books. So how are you liking your stay here?"

"It's been right *gut* so far," he said. "Even better now, after seeing you."

Evelyn couldn't believe it. He was flirting with this *Englisch* woman right in front of her.

Penny blushed even rosier and pushed her glasses up on the bridge of her nose. "I was hoping I'd see you again."

"As I mentioned before, I'm a big fan of libraries. You'll likely see lots of me. Are you about ready, Evelyn?"

Evelyn finished her business quickly and gathered her books. "Thank you, Penny. Let's go, Benjamin."

Benjamin said his goodbyes and they walked out. Evelyn hurried ahead of him.

"Slow down, Evelyn. What's your hurry?" he asked.

"I'm just ready to head home is all." She didn't look at him.

"I thought you'd want to see a little more of the town."

"I need to stop at the grocery, then I should get back." Her voice was a little chilly. Even she could hear it.

"Evelyn?" he said, touching her elbow. "What's wrong with you? Are you mad at me now?"

She whirled to face him. "I'm not mad at you. I just don't like to watch you flirting with fancy women."

Benjamin tipped his head back and laughed. "You think I was flirting."

"*Jah*, I do."

"I wasn't."

"What would you call it then?" she asked, frustrated. "You told Penny your visit was better now that you saw her again."

She had the fleeting thought that she had no call to question him about his actions. He wasn't beholden to her. She felt her cheeks go red.

"I like Penny. She's a nice friendly woman. And she was kind to me when I first got here. She helped me get a library card, and that's been real nice. I got some good books on dairy goat farming just the other day."

Evelyn bit her lip and looked at him. "I don't think that's what she thought you meant. She likes you. I can tell."

"I like her, too, but not in the way you're implying."

She didn't know why a sense of relief washed through her at his words, but she wasn't ready to explore her feelings too closely.

"I don't think she knows that."

"Don't worry. I'll make sure she understands. I was just being nice, Evie."

The nickname made tears sting her eyes. Her mother used to call her Evie but hadn't for a long, long time. The memory made her miss her mother again as if she'd only recently passed.

They got in the buggy and rolled off toward the grocery. A small smile played across Ben's lips as he drove.

"So, if I didn't know better, I'd say you sounded a bit jealous."

"Jealous?" she asked, marveling again at his forward manner. "Don't be silly."

"I said if I didn't know better," he protested.

"Just as long as you do know better," she said, wondering at herself, too. This man seemed to loosen her tongue. Imagine, him even joking about such things.

"Let's just get to the grocery and go home," she said, averting her eyes from his.

Evelyn couldn't get the trip to town out of her mind. She couldn't stop thinking about Ben. He was so aggravating, yet she felt somehow drawn to him. He was always cheerful even when he was teasing and irritating. The twinkle never seemed to leave his eyes, and his dimples danced regularly.

Yet he frustrated her. He could be flippant and nosey, less appealing traits to be sure. Another thing was the way he looked at her. Sometimes, he seemed to peer straight into her soul. It felt like he could see her very thoughts as if she'd written them out for him.

As she got ready for bed that night, she sat on the chair by the window and brushed her hair, the auburn tresses falling nearly to her waist when they were unbound. She gazed out the window as she ran the brush through her hair and noticed the light in the window at the top of the barn.

That was Benjamin's room, she realized. He was there now, probably getting ready to climb into his own bed. She pictured him changing into his nightclothes and splashing water on his face from a pitcher on his nightstand. The image sent a shiver coursing down her spine.

Then he would probably get down on his knees and say his prayers.

Now his head would be bowed, his hands folded. His silky dark hair would curl on the back of his neck. The span of his shoulders was impressive, even in her imagination.

She wondered if he would mention her as he prayed. The thought startled her. Why should he pray for her? It's not like she was an important person in his life. They barely knew each other.

Well, she would pray for him anyway. She would pray he took less pleasure in annoying her and pray for her to have patience with him because he seemed to drain her natural supply.

The next morning, Evelyn gathered the eggs and hummed to herself. It promised to be another crisp sunny day.

She carried the basket of eggs back toward the house but paused to take in the stunning beauty of the sunrise. Violets and corals streaked the horizon, and the first rays of light highlighted the outline of trees and bushes. Across the road was a pasture dotted with maples and oaks and birds singing their morning aria was the only sound to be heard.

Until a roar filled the air.

"Evelyn! Come quick! Dan's been hurt."

# Chapter Seven

Evelyn spun back around to see Benjamin calling her. When he saw he had her attention, he waved her toward him and loped back toward the barn. Evelyn set the basket of eggs down and ran after him, prayers flying up as fast as her feet moved. Farm accidents could be serious, even fatal.

Evelyn burst through the barn door and skidded to a halt. Dan was propped against a hay bale, blood streaking down his face. His leg was stretched at a strange angle in front of him.

"What happened?" she asked, her heartbeat slowing once she saw Dan was conscious.

"He was coming down the ladder and a cat decided to go up at the same time. He tripped over it and fell. He cut his head, and I think his leg is broken."

"Oh, Dan, I'm so sorry you're hurt." She knelt down beside her brother, and he eyed her hazily, his eyes filled with pain.

"He needs to go to the hospital," Ben said. "Can you stay with him while I go tell Rachel what's happened and run to the phone shanty?"

Evelyn nodded, then she stood and whipped off her apron and hurried to the water bucket in a nearby stall. She wet her apron and hurried back to the men. "You go, I'll stay with Dan."

Ben took off and Evelyn once again knelt next to Dan and used the wet apron to wipe the blood from his face. It was a head wound so it was bleeding freely. She sucked her breath in when he winced as she pressed the cleaner edge of the apron on his wound.

"It'll be all right, Dan," she murmured. "Help is on the way."

A couple of moments later, Rachel came running in and hurried over to Dan's side.

"Oh, Dan, sweetheart, what's happened?"

"I-I'll be all right," he stammered. "I'm sorry, Rach. I know this is going to be hard on you."

"Don't talk silly. I'm just grateful you'll be okay."

Just then Ben came back in carrying Mary and holding Teddy's hand. Both children looked frightened and pale.

Evelyn moved quickly to wrap her arms around Teddy and gave Mary a warm, reassuring smile.

"Don't worry, *kinner*," she said, "help is on the way for your father. He's going to be fine."

"I've made the phone call. I told the little ones their father would be fine, but they had to see for themselves," Ben said. "So I brought them down here. I hope that was okay."

"Of course," Rachel said, "they need to see life is full of ups and downs, but the *gut* Lord is always here protecting us."

"*Jah*," Ben said, setting Mary down so she could run to her father's side. Teddy, too, moved to stand closer to Dan.

"Don't worry, *kinner*," he said, "your *daed* is going to be up and going again real soon."

Rachel stood and took control of the situation. "Ben, will you hitch up the buggy, and I'll go into town after the ambulance takes Dan there. Evelyn, will you stay with the *kinner* while I'm gone?"

"Of course," Evelyn answered.

"And I'll drive you into town," Ben said. "Hey, I hear the ambulance coming now."

Soon the transport was parked, and two men and a woman swarmed in and took over. They worked swiftly and loaded Dan onto a gurney and were soon on their way, siren wailing. Ben and Rachel climbed into the buggy and took off, too.

Evelyn took one of each child's hands in her own and led them toward the house.

"You two haven't had breakfast yet, have you? I think we should do something about that." They walked into the kitchen and Evelyn moved to the stove. "How about pancakes?"

They both nodded eagerly, and she moved to get started. She chatted brightly as she worked and gave the kids little tasks to keep their minds busy. She sat a plate filled with small pancakes on the table and they all took their places and bowed their heads.

The *kinner* were quiet as they ate, and Evelyn knew they were worried about their *daed*. She was, too. She didn't think the head wound was serious, but she was no doctor.

"Let's say a special prayer for *daed*," she said. She held the hands of the little ones and prayed out loud. "Dear *Gott, denki* for taking care of *Daed* at the hospital and bringing him home to us soon. Please let him heal well and guide the doctors' hands as they work with him."

Two little voices echoed her "amen."

"Now, let's get this kitchen all cleaned up for *Maem* before she gets home, okay?"

They worked together to wash the dishes and straighten up the room. "Now let's go see if we can finish some of the chores for Ben and *Daed*, okay? Get your jackets."

They went out to the barn and Evelyn discovered, thankfully, that the goats had already been milked. The stalls still needed cleaning, and a few animals still had to be fed. Evelyn set to work. She gave Teddy the task of pushing the broom around the barn floor and set Mary on a bale of hay and put her in charge of watching the kittens.

Evelyn fed the animals and let them out into the pasture. Then she went back into the barn and grabbed a pitchfork and started cleaning stalls. First the horses', then the cows', then the goats'. She started singing a song as she worked, hoping the *kinner* would enjoy the silly ditty.

It was hard work, and she was soon sweating in spite of the temperature, but she kept cleaning and singing. She'd put on a clean apron after the ambulance left, but it was already streaked with dirt. Her cheeks were rosy with exertion, her face damp with perspiration, but her voice rang clear and true as she finished the song.

The sound of applause from behind startled Evelyn, and she turned quickly to find Ben standing there.

"Lovely, Evelyn. That was lovely."

Evelyn felt her face flame red. The song was for the kids, not a grown man.

"Besides having a beautiful singing voice, it looks like you're a pretty good stall cleaner, too," he remarked with a grin.

Evelyn shoved a lock of hair that had come loose from under her *kapp* back with her hand. "*Denki*. Now, how is my brother?"

"He's in surgery for his leg. Rachel is going to spend the day and likely the night with him. They think he'll be able to come home in the morning. She hopes you don't mind staying with the kids."

"Of course not. So Dan will be all right?"

"He should be. He's gotten some stitches in his forehead and won't be able to get around too well for a bit, but they think he'll be fine in the long run."

"*Denki, Gott*," Evelyn said, closing her eyes with relief.

"Now, let me take over the stall cleaning. Looks like you're almost done." He winked at her and held out his hand for the pitchfork.

He had *winked* at her. The familiarity of the man shocked her. She shook her head, gathered the *kinner*, and strode back to the house.

# Chapter Eight

Evelyn spent the afternoon making an apple cobbler. The house was filled with the rich aroma of baking apples and spices when she turned her attention to putting together a big pot of chili for supper. She was browning the hamburger when Ben came in the back door.

"It smells downright sinful in here."

"Supper won't be ready for a while yet," she told him.

"I know. I came to see if I can give you a hand."

Evelyn's eyes widened. A man offering to help in the kitchen? That was unusual.

"Are you serious?" she asked.

"*Jah*, I am. My *maem* insisted that all her sons learn to cook. 'There's no guarantee you'll always have a woman', she said."

"Your *maem* sounds like a smart woman."

"Oh, she is smart. She had all boys and taught them all to cook and clean and even sew a seam. I remember one time I was sewing a seam in my shirt, and I stood up, and the shirt was sewn to my pants. We had a good laugh over that one. Now, what can I do to help?"

"Could you chop up an onion for me? I laid it there on the counter."

"Of course. So, tell me about your family."

Evelyn smiled as she remembered the happy times of her childhood. "My *daed* is big and strong. He's a carpenter. My *maem* was a beautiful person who loved to bake and quilt. She died when I was twelve."

"I'm sorry. That must have been hard for you."

Evelyn shrugged and blinked back tears, picturing her mother's face in her mind. She had been so kind and patient, such a hard worker—even when cancer started winning its battle. She was so different from Greta.

"It was *Gott's* choice to call her home. I had three older brothers, a father, and a home to take care of. I missed her, though. I missed her a lot. I still do."

"So why did you leave home and come here?"

Evelyn stirred the hamburger and turned to get the colander, so she could drain it. Was he just being nosey again or did he really want to know? She glanced at him and saw he was watching her with a compassionate look on his face.

"My brothers are all married with families of their own, and my father recently remarried. I needed to get away for a bit. What about you? You were seeing the wrong woman it seemed?"

Benjamin ran his hand through his dark hair. "I was seeing a woman my mother and father didn't approve of. She was *Englisch,* so I guess that goes without saying. They thought it was best if I had a little more space to think about it, so *Maem* asked Cousin Rachel if I could come here for a while."

"And you said you like it here, right?"

"Right. I like working with the goats and being more independent than I was at home. I was the youngest of five boys, so the farm isn't big enough to support us all. I worked at the RV factory but was laid off, so I agreed to come here."

Evelyn studied him closely. He didn't seem particularly heartbroken about the decision to leave his woman behind.

"Did you ... love her?" She blushed when she asked the question. Now, who was being nosey.

"I'm not sure," he said quietly. "I thought I did but staying with her would have meant leaving the Amish. I didn't want to do that."

Evelyn nodded and didn't say anything. She added the onions to the pan and stirred, thinking about what he had said. She couldn't imagine leaving the church. It was the only life she knew; it was the life she loved.

"Where are the *kinner?*" he asked.

"In the living room coloring," she answered. "I better go check on them."

"*Nee,* let me," he said and walked out of the room.

When he hadn't come back a few minutes later, Evelyn peeked into the living room. He sat cross-legged on the floor, coloring a page in a coloring book and talking to the *kinner*. The sight brought a smile to her face. They all looked cozy and content.

The forthcoming evening went surprisingly well. Benjamin was polite and pleasant to spend time with. He even helped Evelyn clean up the kitchen after they'd finished eating the chili and the grilled peanut butter sandwiches she'd made.

He stayed after supper and played with the *kinner*. He was down on his knees running a wooden horse across the floor when she announced it was time for the *kinner* to go to bed.

Teddy looked disappointed, but he got up reluctantly and gathered his toys. A light came into his eyes, and he turned to look at Ben.

"Will you tuck me in, *Onkel* Ben?" he asked, his chocolate brown eyes big and appealing.

Ben looked startled, but a slow grin spread across his face. "I'd be happy, too, little buddy."

Teddy beamed and slipped his small hand into Ben's big one like he'd done it a thousand times before, and they headed up the stairs.

"I guess that leaves me and you, missy," Evelyn said to Mary, and they followed in Ben and Teddy's footsteps.

Evelyn and Mary went up the stairs to the little girl's bedroom, and Evelyn helped her change into her nightgown. She brushed the blonde locks of the little girl, and then braided the silken tresses.

"Okay, time for prayers," she told Mary, and the little girl dropped to her knees. Evelyn joined her and folded her hands.

"Dear *Gott*, thank you for helping *Daed* today. I hope he comes home soon." She paused, then continued thoughtfully. "And thanks for letting Eblyn be here and Ben, too. I wish they could live here forever."

Mary's innocent words shook Evelyn. *Live here forever?* With Ben? She didn't know whether the idea appalled her or appealed to her. The evening had been pleasant as she and Ben worked together to get supper on the table and clean the kitchen afterward. He had whistled as he dried the dishes and told stories of his childhood. They had actually gotten along. He hadn't irritated her all evening.

It had almost been like they were a true couple, and Teddy and Mary were their own *kinner*.

But the idea of them both being here forever? It was absurd.

Wasn't it?

# Chapter Nine

Evelyn snuck out early the next morning and gathered the eggs then quickly slipped back into the house. By the time Benjamin came in for breakfast, she had bacon, eggs, fried potatoes, and biscuits made.

"Morning, Evelyn," he said, coming in and removing his hat. "The milking's done and I'm hungry as a bear."

"*Gut*, because I've made plenty. Teddy and Mary helped set the table, and we're ready to eat.

"I am a little later than usual since I didn't have Dan's help with the chores. I guess I won't for a while. He's going to be laid up for a bit."

"Don't worry. I'll pitch in and help. Rachel will be home to care for the *kinner*."

"That would be great, but you don't have to if you don't want to. I can handle it."

"*Nee,* I want to."

"I'll go into town after a bit and check on Dan and Rachel. Hopefully, they'll be ready to come home by then."

"I hope so. Now, get washed up, and let's eat."

Later that morning, Ben took the buggy and went to town. While he was gone, Evelyn gave the house an extra cleaning and baked chocolate chip cookies. They used to be Dan's favorite, and she hoped they still were.

It was early afternoon when she heard the buggy rolling up the drive. Peering out the window, she saw it was Ben, Dan, and Rachel.

"They're back," she hollered to the kids, then headed outdoors to greet her brother and sister-in-law.

"Welcome home," she cried. "How are you feeling, Dan?"

Her brother still looked pale beneath his weather-toughened skin, and there were stitches across his forehead, but he managed a grin as Ben helped him from the buggy. "I'm *gut* and glad to be home. The hospital isn't a place you want to be."

"Here, let me take your things." She reached out and took the bag of supplies the hospital had sent home with Rachel. Dan was on crutches and Rachel hovered beside him, ready to catch him if he wobbled. After the children latched onto their mother, the group made their way into the house.

"Sit, sit," she urged Dan. "Let me get you some *kaffee* and cookies."

They all sat and chatted for a few minutes, but Dan was obviously worn out.

"Come on, dear, let's get you in bed," Rachel said to him, then said over her shoulder, "I'll be right back. Wait for me, please. I'd like to talk to you both."

Ben reached for another cookie while they waited. "These are so *gut*, I could eat a dozen of them."

Evelyn smiled as she poured him more *kaffee*. She was glad he liked her baking.

Rachel returned a few minutes later. She, too, looked tired and drawn.

"Are you okay, Rachel? You look like you're done in," Evelyn said.

"I am tired, but I'm fine," she said, taking her seat at the table again. "How did you two get by last night?"

"Right fine," Ben said and smiled. "Your sister-in-law is a *gut* cook."

Rachel chuckled. "I should have known that would be important to you, Ben. Anyway, there's something I want to talk to you two about."

"What is it, Rachel? It's not bad news, is it?" Evelyn asked, her brow furrowing.

"Oh, it's not bad at all. You see, Dan and I promised the *kinner* we would take them to the Winter Festival this weekend, but now I don't think Dan will be up to it. I was wondering if you two could take them for us."

Evelyn lowered her gaze for a moment to think. Of course, she wanted to help Dan and Rachel, but she felt uneasy about spending more time alone with just Ben and the *kinner*. Last night had felt almost too good, too comfortable, as if they were a real family. She'd wanted a family of her own for as long as she could remember. Those hopes were dwindling now that Mark King and she were growing apart.

But she didn't know if she wanted to turn her attention to Ben just because she and Mark were no longer seeing each other. Her first impression of Ben had been that he was a bit trivial and arrogant, and he liked annoying her. Yet, she was wondering if she had judged him too quickly.

Truth be told, if she were honest, she had to admit she was attracted to him. He was undeniably good-looking. His eyes were captivating, magnetizing. She felt a bit wobbly when she looked into their clear, ice-blue depths.

But she wasn't sure how she felt about Ben. Conflicting emotions were warring within her. And she couldn't put down the fact that he was clearly intrigued by *Englisch* women. That couldn't be good.

"Evelyn? Will that be okay with you? Ben said he's willing to do it. What about you?"

"*J-jah,* I will go then," she agreed a bit reluctantly. "I want to be helpful, Rachel."

"*Denki.* I hate to let the *kinner* down. That will be a big help." Rachel reached across the table and covered Evelyn's hand.

"It's a date then. We'll settle the details later," Ben said, studying her closely.

She nodded but didn't respond. A *date?* That sounded too odd when it came to her and Ben. A few days ago, she could hardly stand the man.

Rachel dusted her hands and stood up. "Okay, that's settled. I didn't get much sleep last night, so I'm going to go lie down for a bit, all right? Do you need anything before I go?"

"*Nee.* You go and get some rest. I'll take care of the *kinner* and make supper." Evelyn stood up. "I'm going to get started mopping this floor now. Ben, you have work to do, too, I'm sure."

"*Jah,* I do. I'll go get started on it." He stood and went out the back door, whistling as he left.

"*Denki*, Evelyn. I appreciate everything you're doing to help out," Rachel told her warmly.

"I'm happy to do it," Evelyn said, but she wasn't sure she meant it. Spending too much time with Ben was simply too confusing.

# Chapter Ten

The next morning dawned gray and wet. Rain drizzled down from a leaden sky and a damp fog settled over the land. Evelyn pulled on her rubber boots and a slicker before she slogged out to the barn to help Ben with the chores. She wasn't looking forward to working alone with him, but she had promised to help, and she wouldn't go back on her word.

"Morning, Evie," Ben called as she entered the barn. "Ready to be a goat farmer?"

"Why not?" she said drolly. "It's a dream come true."

Ben laughed and said, "Well, *gut*. I already sterilized the equipment, so let's get the milking done."

Evelyn had milked cows before but never a goat.

"It's not a lot different," Ben assured her as they led the first goat into the milking stall. "Put some alfalfa in the box, and then have a seat on the stool." He went on to explain they needed to clean the goat's teats before milking. "The first stream should be caught in a separate cup. It's the most likely to contain bacteria. Then you wipe the teat with a paper towel before resuming milking."

Evelyn was amazed by his patience as he taught her the fundamentals. He never raised his voice or showed any impatience if she fumbled. When she had difficulty getting the milk stream started, he knelt beside her and gently covered her hands with his own.

"Move your hand up a bit and don't tug on the teat, just squeeze it."

The stream splashed into the bucket, and Evelyn squealed with excitement. "I did it!"

Ben laughed and gave her hand an extra squeeze as their gazes locked. She felt as if she'd fallen into the warm blue pools that were his eyes. His black lashes surrounded the twinkling cornflower blue pupils, and her breath caught in her throat.

She managed to break the spell when she asked, "What's next?"

He paused a moment before he answered. "Now, you keep milking until her udder is almost empty."

"Okay, I can do that."

They finished the milking then tackled the rest of the chores. Once again, they worked well together, chatting at times, working in harmonious silence at other times. She was still amazed they could be together without him asking nosey questions or teasing her about something. He was actually a nice man sometimes.

"There," he said. "We're done. *Gut* job. Let's go eat breakfast."

Evelyn flexed her tired shoulders and nodded in agreement. The hard work had definitely whetted her appetite. "This time, I'm so hungry I could eat a bear."

"Sorry, I don't think bear is on the menu this morning. Will you settle for bacon and eggs?"

"Almost anything sounds good to me," she admitted with a grin. "Let's go see what we're having."

They were laughing about something Ben said as they walked into the kitchen, and Rachel turned to smile at them.

"Are you two hungry?' she asked.

"We are," Evelyn said. "What do you need help with?"

If you'll just pour some *kaffee* for you two, we're all set. I'm going to take a tray in for Dan. You two go ahead."

"Okay. I'll dish up the food for us and the *kinner*," Evelyn said. She looked over her shoulder as Rachel left the room, then took note of the pan of scrambled eggs and the pot of oatmeal.

She looked at Ben and said with a pout, "No bear."

"Maybe next time," he said consolingly, and they both burst out laughing.

Later that morning, Evelyn was sweeping the front porch. The rain had stopped, and the temperature was slowly climbing. She enjoyed the fresh-washed smell of the earth after the rain and hummed softly as she swept. She looked over as the door opened, and Rachel joined her on the porch.

"The kids are sitting with their *daed,* and he's reading them a story," she said. "I wanted to tell you I'm glad you and Benjamin are getting along better."

Evelyn stopped sweeping and gazed at Rachel. She was getting along with him better, but she didn't know how she really felt about him.

"Well, he hasn't asked any personal questions lately or made me drop eggs on my feet, anyway."

Rachel chuckled and said, "It sounds like he's making progress. Is he growing on you as I predicted?"

Evelyn scoffed. "Like a mushroom," she said then smiled. She hated to admit it, but he was becoming more palatable. She had enjoyed spending time with him last night and this morning. He carried on an easy conversation and did have a good sense of humor.

"Okay, I do like him better than I did, I admit it. I still have my doubts about him, though. He didn't make a very good first impression."

He deserves a second chance, though, don't you think? He's pretty special to me," Rachel said. "You know, he saved my life when I was ten."

"You never told me that. What happened?"

"I was being silly and went sliding on an ice-covered pond. Unfortunately, it turned out that the ice wasn't very thick, and I fell through. Ben pulled me out with a tree limb. There was a big chance he'd fall in, too. When he got me out, he wrapped me in his coat. I would have drowned if he hadn't acted so quickly."

Evelyn pictured the scene in her mind. Rachel would have been soaking wet and shivering. Ben would have been cold, too, but he had given up his coat to keep Rachel warm. Such a gallant gesture. It made her heart melt a bit as she thought about it.

"I can see why you care so much about him," she said.

"*Jah*, I do. I still think he might be attracted to you, Evelyn."

Evelyn's cheeks flamed, and she went back to sweeping the floor, averting her gaze from Rachel's. She didn't think that was true. He was just a garrulous fellow who enjoyed life, and he seemed to have never met a stranger.

"Well, I'm not attracted to him," she finally said.

*Jah, and lying is a sin,* she scolded herself. She had to admit that she was attracted to him, despite her stubbornness. There was something about him that drew her.

She wasn't ready for Rachel to know that, though.

# Chapter Eleven

The Saturday of the festival came before she knew it. Evelyn was glad the kids would be with her and Benjamin this afternoon. Otherwise, she feared it would be too awkward.

She'd gone upstairs to check her hair and put on a clean dress and apron. She'd prayed for rain so they would have a good excuse not to go, but apparently, she wasn't going to get her way. Even the *kinner* would have understood then. But unfortunately, the clear winter day was beautiful.

She went downstairs where the *kinner* waited eagerly for her, their faces alight with excitement. Benjamin lounged on the sofa where Dan was sitting with his leg propped on a stool. He stood when Evelyn appeared, a child now holding onto each of her hands.

"Looks like everyone's ready to go, Dan. We'll see you when we get back. Don't run any races while we're gone," Ben said with a chuckle.

The children let loose of Evelyn's hands and went racing outside to the buggy. They were already seated by the time Evelyn and Ben caught up with them. In the buggy, Ben clicked to the horse. "We're off."

"Yeah! We're off!" the children echoed Ben's words and gave a little cheer. Evelyn couldn't stop the smile their excitement brought to her face.

"We'll be there in time for the parade," Ben announced. "I love a *gut* parade."

She smiled. He seemed almost as excited as the *kinner*. The weather was perfect for enjoying a parade. The sky was a breathtaking shade of sapphire blue and billowy soft puffs of white clouds floated effortlessly across the serene surface. The sun was warm on her cheeks and a cool breeze tickled her nose.

The trip to town passed quickly, and soon they were hitching the horse to a post in the parking lot of the park. People swarmed along the sidewalks, and cars crawled along the crowded streets. Evelyn took Mary's hand, and Ben took Teddy's before they started maneuvering their way through the teeming throng.

"This is quite a crowd for little Shiloh Creek," Evelyn said.

"Dan told me the festival draws people from far and wide. He thinks we'll be ready to sell our goats' milk cheese and other products here by the spring festival. Rachel's going to try her hand at making soap from the milk, too."

"That sounds interesting. I wish I were staying longer so I could help her."

He looked at her and raised his eyebrow curiously. "How long are you staying?"

"I don't know. When I came here, I was stressed and didn't have any real plan. I just wanted to get away for a while."

"Do you like it here?"

"I do. The people seem friendly, the area is pretty, but that's true at home, too. I do miss *Daed,* but, I don't know. I don't see much of a future for me there."

"There's no one special waiting for you?"

She thought about Mark, but knew he wasn't the answer. She'd only been seeing him for so long because she had hoped she would get past the things she didn't really like about him. Now she knew that wasn't going to happen. The way he cracked his knuckles whenever he felt a bit of stress made her jaw tighten just thinking about it. He had a bit of a superior attitude that bothered her, too.

She looked at Ben and shook her head. "*Nee*, no one special. I was seeing someone, but it didn't work out."

Just then the sound of an approaching band filled the air, and the *kinner* leapt with excitement. They all moved to the edge of the street and watched as the Shiloh Creek High School band marched into view and played a lively song.

Evelyn loved watching the faces of the *kinner* as they watched the band pass by, along with the other parade participants of little league teams, Scouts, and Future Farmers of America. Mary and Teddy laughed with delight when the cheerleaders walked by waving and tossing out candy, and they cheered as the fire trucks went by with sirens wailing.

She felt Ben poke her in the ribs and turned toward him. He grinned and pointed at a toddler next to him who danced along with the blaring music. It was cuteness overload, and Evelyn laughed along with Ben as they watched the happy child.

A man on stilts tottered by, and a group of teenagers riding unicycles waved as they rolled past. Evelyn was grateful there was no ice on the street, or neither would have been possible. The parade went on nearly an hour. Ben bought them all lemon shakeups, and they munched on the candy the *kinner* collected from parade participants. When it was finally over, even Evelyn felt a bit of disappointment.

Afterward, they wandered amongst the booths and eyed the displays. The children were allowed to pull plastic ducks from a stream of water and each one earned a small prize before they strolled over and checked out the displays of goods for sale.

"You know, I think a stand of goats' milk products would do well here," Evelyn said thoughtfully, her mind spinning with ideas. "I wonder how much milk it takes to make a batch of soap?"

"I'm sure you can get some books at the library that will walk you through the process," Ben suggested.

"Could I get some ice cream?" Teddy begged.

"I think that could be arranged," Ben said. "Let's go."

By the time they headed home, the little ones were worn out. They fell asleep in the back of the buggy almost immediately after they climbed in.

Ben guided the horse down the road and turned his head to look at Evelyn. "I had a nice time today. *Denki* for coming with me."

The sincerity of his tone surprised Evelyn. Many men wouldn't have bothered to thank her for doing something her brother and sister-in-law had suggested. A sense of warmth swam through her.

"*Denki* for saying so, Ben. I appreciate it."

The evening was beautiful. The horse's hooves clopped rhythmically along the road and their percussion was accompanied by a chorus of owl hoots. A faraway cow lowed, and the sun started to fall slowly toward the horizon.

Evelyn sighed with contentment. She did like it here.

"Did you notice the feeling of being family today?" he asked.

"*Jah*, Ben, I did. We shouldn't get used to that, though. We'll probably both leave someday soon." She played with the strings of her *kapp* as she spoke.

"I don't think I will. Dan and I have talked about joining forces. He will do more of the agricultural side of things, and I'll manage the goats and business side. I think we'll make a *gut* team."

Evelyn nodded thoughtfully. She thought Rachel and she would make a good team, too. The thought of the goat's milk soap-making business intrigued her.

The dogs came to greet them as the buggy turned into the driveway at home. Evelyn noticed right away that there was an unfamiliar red convertible parked in the drive.

"I wonder whose car that is?" she said as they approached.

"I know who it belongs to," he said, his voice tight.

"Who?"

"It's Wendy Powell's, the *Englisch* woman I was seeing back home."

# Chapter Twelve

Ben pulled the buggy up beside the porch, and they roused the children. Evelyn felt a little queasy as she helped the kids into the house. Wendy Powell's arrival was completely unexpected and somehow made her feel threatened. This woman had had a relationship with Ben. Evelyn didn't know how special it had been, but the idea of their closeness wasn't a happy one.

Evelyn stepped into the kitchen and found Dan, Rachel, and a striking blonde woman sitting at the table. She felt tension in the air when she entered, but maybe that was just her own nerves.

"Evelyn, this is Wendy Powell. Wendy, my sister Evelyn." Dan stood and made the introductions, but she noticed he wasn't smiling.

"Hello," Wendy said, "it's nice to meet you. Where's Benny?"

*Benny?* Evelyn wanted to snort, but she controlled herself.

"Benny is in the barn tending the horse," she said, catching a grin slide across Dan's face.

"Is it all right if I go out there and see him?" she asked, her blue eyes wide.

"*Jah*, you may. Would you like me to show you the way?" Dan asked.

"No, that's okay. I'll find it."

"You might need a flashlight. Let me get you one."

Rachel moved to retrieve a flashlight.

"No, that's okay. I've got my phone." She held up a cell phone in her hand. "It has a flashlight app I can use."

"Oh. Just take the path straight out to the barn."

Wendy headed out the door. Evelyn stared after her. Wendy was wearing blue jeans and a light pink jacket. She'd probably get chilly out there. Maybe she should take her an extra jacket? No, she was a grown woman. She could take care of herself.

"Evelyn, a letter came for you today. I think it's from your *daed*." Rachel held out an envelope, completely ignoring the entire subject of their *Englisch* visitor.

"*Denki*, Rachel. I'll help you get the *kinner* to bed then read it."

She held Mary's hand as they went up the stairs, listening to her chatter about the day. She tucked the little girl into bed then went to her own room and tore open the envelope containing her father's letter. She sat in the chair by the window and glanced out toward the barn hoping to see some sign of Ben and his visitor. When she saw no one, she read the contents of her letter.

Her father wanted her to come home. He said Greta had been having a hard time with her pregnancy, and they could use her help.

Why did that not surprise her? Greta was still up to her old tricks. If Evelyn thought for a moment that Greta truly was having difficulty, she would have already gone back. But she instinctively knew Greta's difficulties were manufactured.

Guilt washed over Evelyn as she crumpled the letter in her hands. She did know her *daed* missed her and wanted her at home, but in truth, she didn't want to go.

She sighed. Greta wasn't likely taking care of *Daed* as she should. Was he getting proper meals? Was the house being kept clean? Had the chickens been seen to?

All these questions bounced around in her head as she gazed again out the window, her attention going once again toward the barn. Was Wendy still there? Of course, she was. Her car still sat boldly in the drive. She could see the moon reflecting off the bright red. What were they doing out there? What were they talking about?

Was he … kissing her? That question poked at Evelyn painfully as she pictured the curvaceous blonde wrapped in Ben's arms, their lips touching. The mere thought sent a shiver of distaste through her.

She forced herself to stop staring out the window at the barn. She needed to decide about going home. She would at least like to stay until Rachel had her baby. She really did need Evelyn's help whereas she wasn't so sure about Greta—at least right now.

Hmm. She would have to think about it.

Evelyn made her way to the barn the next morning to help with the chores. She didn't feel eager to work with Ben, but there was no getting out of it.

They didn't talk much as they worked quietly and steadily until they were finished.

"Are you coming in for breakfast?" she asked.

"*Jah*, I'll be there in a minute."

Evelyn stopped to gather the eggs on her way back to the house. Ben had seemed a bit troubled this morning. He was missing his usual sparkle, and there were lines of fatigue around his eyes. Maybe he had been up all night with Wendy, she thought spitefully, reaching for another egg.

She knew that wasn't true because she'd been watching and had seen Wendy's car drive away late last night, but the thought crept through her mind anyway. Why was she such a cynical person nowadays, she wondered? She needed to work on that.

Evelyn went back to the house, and they had breakfast, Ben eating and escaping just as quickly. Evelyn ate then hurried through the morning chores. She wanted to spend some time in the outside this morning.

She went out to the frozen garden plot that Dan had cleaned up before his accident. But he hadn't quite finished and since it wasn't too cold, she decided to clear the rest of the weeds.

Now, she was vigorously working the hoe, chopping mercilessly at any weed that had dared to show its head above the hard ground. The sun was warm on her head as she worked, and she paused for a moment to take in the scenery around her.

Everything was quite barren looking, though it sparkled when the low sunshine hit bits of icy patches. In the distance, the river rolled past, sunlight sparkling on the surface.

This was such a beautiful place, so peaceful and serene. Even the sound of the goats bleating in the background was soothing. In the distance, she could hear the mournful wail of a train as it passed through the countryside.

"Leaning on that hoe doesn't accomplish much, you know," a voice suddenly said from behind her.

Evelyn whirled and saw Benjamin standing behind her, and heat flamed in her cheeks. He'd caught her daydreaming.

"Just enjoying the day," she said.

"*Jah*, it is lovely. This is my favorite time of year. Everything is resting but gearing up for a fresh start come spring. It is the mystical cycle of life."

"It is lovely," Evelyn said. "I marvel at every season."

He eyed her curiously. "Is it ... like a spiritual experience for you? It is for me."

Her voice caught in her throat as she felt his gaze upon her, so she simply nodded. She didn't think she could talk when those blue eyes of his studied her so closely. She broke off their locked gazes and started hoeing again. She didn't want to have such an intimate conversation with him. His eyes already seared her soul. She needed to change the subject.

"Did you enjoy your visit with Wendy last night?" She flinched after she asked the question. She hadn't meant to bring the subject of Wendy up. *Ach*, but what was she thinking?

"It was nice to see an old friend from home," he said quietly. "Wendy and I worked together at the RV plant. We got to be good friends."

"I'm sorry. That was me being nosey. I shouldn't have asked. It's none of my business."

"No, it's all right. There's no reason you shouldn't ask. It was hard to see her again, though. At one time, I thought I might ... well, I wanted to marry her."

She heard the pain in his voice as he said the words, and a cramp caught her heart. It hurt her to think of him marrying another woman, especially an *Englisch* woman. If he did that, he would have to leave the church. He could no longer remain Amish. She couldn't imagine him being anything other than Amish.

"Was it ... a hard decision to let her go?" she asked quietly.

He shook his head. "It was an impossible situation. I'm Amish. I will always be Amish. I wouldn't want it any other way."

He said the words, tugged on the brim of his hat, and walked away.

# Chapter Thirteen

Evelyn received another letter from her father the next day. He asked her again to come home, and once again she was torn. She didn't want to go, but she feared she was being selfish. And her father needed her. Maybe he could hold off just a little longer. Rachel's baby was due in just a couple more weeks. Greta's wasn't due for quite some time. Hopefully, she could be of help for both babies. She decided to write her father and ask.

She and Rachel were making vegetable soup for supper when Evelyn brought up the subject. Rachel's face fell when Evelyn mentioned going home.

"I would hate to see you go, Evelyn. Not just because you're such a big help, either." Rachel said as she chopped a stalk of celery. "I do think we would make a great team in the goat milk soap niche, and I love your company."

"*Denki*, Rachel. I feel exactly the same. And, as ashamed as I am to admit it, I do think Greta's main goal is to get her personal servant back."

"You might be right. *Ach*, but we mustn't gossip. We should give her the benefit of the doubt."

"*Jah*, you're right. I'm going to try harder when I do return home. Sometimes, I am quite disappointed with myself." Evelyn picked up another potato and started slicing it. She needed to make a decision soon. Her father needed her, but there was a part of her that wanted to stay here. Regrettably, she knew part of the reason she was reluctant to go home was because she secretly wanted to see if her feelings for Ben might lead to a deeper relationship between them. Feelings she hadn't even admitted to herself she was having.

After church that Sunday, Evelyn decided to go for a walk. She wanted to be alone for a while to gather her scattered thoughts. She strolled down to the river and began following a path that had been worn along the banks.

She'd always loved being near the water. River or lake, it didn't matter. She just enjoyed a sense of serenity when she was within sight of water.

Evelyn rounded a bend in the path and stopped to take in the sight. Large trees bordered the banks, and a small waterfall tumbled playfully across a little ledge. The sound was like a quiet symphony tinkling melodiously.

A large rock on the riverbank beckoned to her and she wandered over to it and took a seat on the hard surface. She gazed down into the gurgling water and enjoyed the beauty of the moment. The day wasn't too cold and there wasn't any wind. In truth, it was unnaturally warm. All remnants of ice and snow were long melted.

Temptation plied her. Wouldn't it feel good to dip her feet into the cool water? Would it be too cold? She giggled, feeling excitement at challenging herself.

She glanced around. She was completely alone. What would it hurt if she slipped off her shoes and stockings and dipped her feet in the water? If it was too painfully cold, she could always put her shoes and socks right back on.

Evelyn quickly took off her shoes and slipped off her stockings. She hiked her skirt well above her ankles and dangled her feet off the edge of the rock and let the water swirl past her ankles. A surprised cry escaped her as she felt the coldness of the water.

"That looks crazy. Mind if I join you?"

Ben's voice from behind her startled her, and she jerked her skirt back down. She hadn't heard him come close.

"It's awful cold," she admitted. "And not a very *gut* idea."

She pulled her feet from the water, stifling a shiver.

"You have surprised me, Evelyn. I must confess that not many Amish girls surprise me." He moved to sit next to her on the boulder. "It's lovely here. I found this spot a couple of weeks ago."

She bent down and quickly put her shoes and socks back on.

"I like to come here to think," he continued.

"I think it's a *gut* spot for it. "

"Have you got something special on your mind you need to think about, Evie?" he asked softly.

"*Nee,* not really," she replied then contradicted herself. "*Jah,* I guess I do. I got a letter from *Daed* asking me to come home. My stepmother is expecting, and he says she's having a rough time.

He looked at her thoughtfully for a minute then concluded, "You don't look too happy about it."

Evelyn wrapped her fingers together in her lap. She didn't want to speak badly of Greta, but she didn't know what to do.

"Greta is about my age. She's never taken care of a household. I was hoping if I was gone for a while, she'd learn to take care of the house and the meals herself."

"And apparently that hasn't happened."

She shook her head. "It doesn't seem so, and I think maybe I shouldn't have left. But I also want to be here to help Rachel when her *boppli* comes."

He leaned forward and dangled his hands between his knees. "It sounds like you need to do more than thinking. Maybe you need to do some praying, too."

She looked into his soft blue eyes and nodded. She did need to pray. She needed to pray for guidance and wisdom as she made this decision.

As she sat there next to Benjamin, she realized she needed to pray about their relationship as well. There was something about him that pulled at her heart. She was surprised how much the thought of leaving him bothered her.

She studied him from under downcast eyelids. His dark hair curled on his neck and his profile was clean and strong. His hands, resting on his knees now, drew her attention. Long, slender fingers, little dark hairs curling on his knuckles. Would his touch make her weak in the knees?

Evelyn jerked her thoughts away from such a topic. Her face grew warm, and she feared she was blushing.

"I've got to go," she said abruptly.

"*Nee,* I can go so you can be alone." She shook her head, so he continued. "I'll see you at later then."

She nodded and turned away. She needed to get away from him and fast.

# Chapter Fourteen

The next day was laundry day. Evelyn and Rachel washed a few loads then hauled baskets of laundry out to the line. Even in the coldest weather, Rachel preferred the outside line. They hung everything up to dry then went back to the house to make lunch.

"Rachel, you look a little pale," Evelyn said as she washed the dishes. "Are you feeling all right?"

"I'm fine, just a little tired." Rachel rubbed her lower back with both hands.

"I think you need to lie down and take a nap," Evelyn told her. "You need a little extra rest right now."

"Maybe in a little while," Rachel said. "Right now, I'm going to clean out that large hall closet."

"I'll help, and if you get too tired, just say so and go lie down."

"That suits," Rachel replied with a chuckle.

They worked together and were done less than an hour later. Rachel was naturally neat and organized, so it wasn't all that messy.

One thing that didn't go back into the closet was a beautiful, old wooden cradle. They dragged it into Dan's and Rachel's bedroom. Rachel stared at it with eyes filled with tears.

"Rachel, what is it? What's wrong?" Evelyn asked in alarm.

"Nothing's wrong, Evelyn. Everything is fine. I'm just feeling sentimental looking at this cradle. My siblings and I all slept here as newborns and so did Teddy and Mary. It just brings back many memories."

Rachel brushed a hand across damp eyelids and smiled. "You know, I think I'll take you up on that offer to let me take a nap. You sure you don't mind watching the kids?"

"Not a bit. You get some rest now."

Evelyn spent time with the *kinner* straightening their rooms. She glanced out the window from Mary's room and noticed rain clouds building on the horizon. From the looks of those clouds, she needed to check the laundry and bring it in quickly before it started raining.

"Stay here, *kinner*, I'll be back in a few minutes. I need to bring in the laundry."

She hurried downstairs and got the baskets before heading outside. Pulling clothespins as quickly as she could, she moved down the line and dropped the clothes in the baskets. She was reaching up to release a bedsheet when she heard a car crunching up the drive.

Peering around the corner of the sheet, her heart fell when she recognized Wendy's little red convertible. *Again.* The blonde drove straight past her to the barn and climbed out of the driver's seat. She ran her hands over her tumbling locks and tugged at the hem of her skirt before walking into the barn.

What was she doing here? Evelyn wondered. Well, it really wasn't any of her business. She finished collecting the rest of the laundry and hurried up to the back porch just as the first drops of rain hit the ground.

Curiosity ate at her, though, and she turned back to look toward the barn. Wendy emerged from the door, and Ben was right behind her. They both got in the car, and they wheeled around and drove away.

A ball of ice formed in the pit of Evelyn's stomach. She didn't know where they were going or what they were going to do, but she did know she didn't want to watch Benjamin Glick court another woman. Had he changed his mind? Or was Wendy interested in becoming Amish?

Maybe it was time for her to go home.

Evelyn made the decision almost instantaneously. Watching Ben drive away with the woman he said he'd almost married was too disturbing.

Rachel was surprised when Evelyn announced her decision and said she was leaving right away. Evelyn had already walked to the phone shanty and called for a driver to take her home. The *kinner* were upset she was going, and Mary cried when she told her goodbye. Evelyn felt a few tears roll down her own cheeks as she sat in the back of the van carrying her away.

# Chapter Fifteen

Evelyn was now home, yet somehow it didn't feel like home. She felt like a stranger in the house she had grown up in. It all looked the same, but nothing felt the same.

*Daed* was happy to see her, she could tell. He wasn't a talkative man, but he had a certain smile that let her know he was content.

Greta, of course, was thrilled Evelyn was back. The first thing she did was plop down on a chair and begin telling Evelyn how awful she'd been feeling and how Evelyn's coming home was a definite relief.

It didn't seem to have affected her appetite any, Evelyn thought to herself. She'd had seconds of everything of the quick supper Evelyn had put together the night before and had eaten a hearty meal for breakfast, even though she complained the smell of *kaffee* made her sick, and the eggs were too greasy for her taste. She'd eaten every bite, though, and helped herself to an extra biscuit.

Well, she was eating for two. Evelyn shrugged her shoulders and focused on finishing the dishes. She had prayed for patience with Greta, and now she needed to practice it.

Soon, her life had fallen right back in its old pattern. Cook, clean, work outside. She did nearly all the work herself with little help from Greta. She didn't mind, though. Keeping busy helped to keep her from thinking about how much she missed Ben and the rest of the family.

If she were honest with herself, she had to admit she missed Ben most of all. It was the image of his face that floated behind her lids when she was trying to go to sleep; it was his smile she kept remembering. Sometimes it even seemed she even caught a whiff of his manly scent.

Now here she was standing on the front porch with a broom in her hand lost in thoughts of Benjamin again, instead of sweeping the porch. She gave herself a stern scolding and started sweeping vigorously.

The crunch of wheels on gravel caught her attention and she turned to see a car pulling into the drive. It looked like the same Mennonite driver who had brought her home last week. She watched closely as the door opened and a tall, broad-shouldered man got out. He was dressed in Amish clothes and his dark hair curled beneath his hat as he strode toward the porch.

*Ben.*

Had her thoughts conjured him up?

# Chapter Sixteen

"Ben. What are you doing here?"

"I'm here to see you, of course." His eyes twinkled as he stared at her with his hands hanging at his sides. "Why else would I be here?"

"I don't know. Is everything all right? Dan? Rachel? The *kinner?*" Her hand fidgeted with the bodice of her apron as she waited for his answer.

"Everyone is fine, and they miss you."

She was confused. If everything was okay, why had he come all this way to see her?

"Evie, I'm here because I need to talk to you. Can we sit down?"

Evelyn realized she was still gripping the broom in front of her with one hand. She turned and propped it in a corner then led the way to a bench. "Let's sit then. There's no wind out here today."

Ben sat, but he didn't say anything for a couple of moments. Instead, he studied her face intently. She squirmed beneath his direct gaze.

"Evelyn, why did you leave so suddenly?" He reached out as if to touch her, but then he must have thought better of it. "I need to know."

She couldn't look him in the eyes anymore, so she studied the hands she had folded neatly in her lap. "I told you I was thinking about coming home the last time we talked."

"But you weren't sure that was what you wanted to do. What made you decide so suddenly?" He reached out, and this time he did touch her. He used the tip of his finger to raise her chin and make her look into the deep, silver-blue pools of his eyes.

"There you go being nosey again. I don't think that's any of your business."

"And I don't happen to agree with you. Now, tell me why you left so suddenly."

"Fine. You want to know why I left? I'll tell you. I left because I saw you get into the car with Wendy and drive away that day. I was ... upset. Was that what you wanted to hear?" A touch of heat flared on her cheekbones. She blinked desperately, fighting to keep tears from filling her eyes.

"*Ach,* Evie, you got the wrong idea. I didn't go with Wendy to get back together with her. I went to let her know that she and I were definitely over."

Evelyn felt the wind seep out of her. He was going to end the relationship with Wendy that day? Truly?

"You thought you wanted to marry her at one time."

"I did. I was in a bad place back then. I'd been laid off and lost my job. I didn't have much of a future ahead of me. Things were looking pretty bleak."

Evelyn watched him closely.

"But things were even worse for Wendy. She was a young widow all alone. She'd been laid off, too. She didn't have any family to lean on. I felt sorry for her and started hanging out with her. She was fun and exciting, different from all the other women I knew. "

She took in his words. She, too, had been at a place in her life where the future didn't look bright, and she felt like she was facing a dead end.

"Then something changed. I prayed a lot. Could I stand to leave the Amish to be with Wendy?" He shook his head. "I seriously thought about it. But I knew I couldn't do it—like I told you."

He shifted. "I told Wendy I couldn't leave the Amish, and that meant I couldn't be with her. She took it hard. She came the other day to tell me she would become Amish if we stayed together."

Evelyn's heart skipped a beat at his words. Would Wendy really change her entire life to be with him?

"I didn't think she really understood what being Amish would mean. I needed to explain it to her, so I went with her to talk.

"I told her she wouldn't be able to drive around in her snazzy, little red car anymore and that her cell phone would be history. The social media she's so fond of would be a thing of the past, just like electricity. No more air conditioning, no more television, no more email. At first, she said, she would be okay with it, then when we pulled into the Ice Cream Shoppe in town, she broke down crying.

"'I won't be able to get my nails done or color my hair,' she sobbed. 'I can't do it. I just can't do it.'"

"But that wasn't the only reason I didn't want to go through with a relationship with her." He paused and looked at Evelyn, his blue eyes piercing through her staring eyes.

"The real reason was I couldn't stop thinking about you. I couldn't get you off my mind. I had dreams about you, Evie. I've fallen for you."

Evelyn looked at him. He looked vulnerable, so humble. And she melted.

"*Ach,* Ben. Do you mean that?" she breathed.

"I've never meant anything more." He smiled as he held her gaze. "I think we make a great team. We work well together, and I can't think of anyone else I'd rather be with. Come back to Shiloh Creek. Please. Let me court you. Let us plan a future together."

Evelyn didn't know how to put her feelings into words. A sudden, overwhelming peace overcame her. She knew she was destined to spend the rest of her life with this man. Her future no longer looked bleak. She felt a purpose, an energy that had been missing from her life.

She was just about to say she would come back that very day when footsteps sounded on the porch.

"Who is this, *dochder*? Introduce me to your friend."

# Chapter Seventeen

"Hello, *Daed*. This is Rachel's cousin, Benjamin Glick." Rachel felt hot color rise in her cheeks.

Benjamin reached out to shake Edward Lantz's hand. "Good afternoon, sir. I'm pleased to meet you."

"What brings you over this way," Edward asked.

"Your daughter. I'd like to talk to you about that."

"Why don't you walk out to the barn with me, Ben? We can talk there."

Evelyn watched the two men walk away, her stomach clenching with nerves. She couldn't believe this was actually happening. She and Ben were going to plan a future together if everything worked out. They would make a home, have *kinner* of their own. They would start a business selling goats' milk and soap and work together to build a good life.

This morning, her future had looked drab and dreary. Now it was filled with sunshine.

But could she really leave that day? What could be done about Greta? She supposedly was too sick and weak to take on all the housework herself. What if *Daed* objected to Evelyn's returning to Dan's home because she was needed here? She tried not to fret, but tension gnawed at her insides.

She needed to do something. She went back inside the house to the kitchen and started chopping vegetables. She would make soup for their supper. That way she could keep her hands busy, and her mind occupied.

Her thoughts still dwelled on what was going on in the barn, though, and she was searching for solutions to the problem with Greta.

She boiled beef and added the vegetables. She shook pepper and salt into the pot before she added a little garlic and some basil. She opened a jar of tomato sauce she'd canned last summer and dumped it into the soup as well.

Evelyn got a spoon to taste the mixture. It was perfect. Now she needed to make some corn muffins. She was mixing the muffin batter when the back door opened and *Daed* walked in. He was alone.

"Where's Ben?" she asked.

"His driver returned to pick him up as we were finishing our talk. He said he'll see you in another time."

"I see." Disappointment washed over her. He was gone, and she was still here. She'd been hoping to go with him when he went back to Shiloh Creek. Instead, here she was. Had anything really changed? What had they discussed? Had her father stopped their courtship before it had even begun?

"Don't look so disappointed, Evelyn. Everything will work out."

Evelyn raised her gaze to meet her father's. He smiled at her and rubbed his beard. "Have patience, *dochder*." He clearly wasn't going to enlighten her further.

She bit her lower lip as she nodded. Once again, praying for patience moved to the top of her prayer list.

Later that evening, after the dishes were done and the floor swept, *Daed* called her out to the porch.

"I want to talk to you. Has Greta gone to bed already?"

"*Jah*, she said she was tired."

"Well, sit down here a minute, and let's talk things over."

Evelyn sat on a bench and *Daed* leaned back against the porch post, his ankles crossed as he studied her. "So, you like this young man Benjamin?"

"I do, *Daed*, I really do."

"Do you think this is the man *Gott* has selected to be your husband?"

She took a deep breath and nodded. She was becoming more and more sure of it by the moment.

"If it is meant to be, it shall be. Do you think Greta could get by if we had a woman come in a couple of hours a day?"

"I think so. Maybe we should talk to Greta about it." Hope began to flicker within her.

"Ben told me about his plans to partner up with Dan in the goat business. He said you and Rachel were going to make soap, too. That sounds like a fine plan to me." He paused and rested his hand on her shoulder. "Do you think you could stay here until we find someone to come in and help? It shouldn't take more than a few days."

Once again, tears filled her eyes, only this time they were tears of joy. Everything was going to be all right, just like her father had said.

# Epilogue

Evelyn hummed as she held her baby to her breast. The little boy, named Aaron Edward, had been born a month ago. She ran her hand over his silken cap of dark hair, breathing in the sweet newborn smell of him.

She didn't know life could be this perfect. She had been married to Ben for exactly one year today.

When she'd come back to Shiloh Creek it had seemed their November wedding date would never arrive, but time had reversed itself after the wedding. The days were speeding by. During the day, she was busy tending their child, cooking, cleaning, and gardening plus learning to make fine quality goats' milk soap. She and Rachel worked well together, sometimes in Rachel's kitchen, sometimes in the kitchen of the house next door that she and Ben had managed to rent.

At night, she found contentment in her husband's arms. Sometimes, she would wake up in the middle of the night and snuggle close against his side, thanking *Gott* for blessing her with this man.

Rachel and Dan were doing well, too. Their baby was born soon after Evelyn returned, a sweet little girl they had named Elizabeth.

Greta and her father had their baby boy now, too. Evelyn's little half-brother's name was James, and she tried to see him as often as possible. Motherhood seemed to have performed a miracle, and Greta had stepped enthusiastically into the role of mother and wife.

Life was *gut*.

The door opened, and Ben slipped quietly into the room. "Is he asleep yet?" he whispered.

Evelyn nodded and kissed the baby's brow. "I'll put him in his cradle now."

"*Nee*, sit still. I'll do it." Ben gently took the sleeping infant and laid him in his crib, tenderly stroking his hand along the tiny back.

"Are you ready for bed then?" he asked turning toward her.

"*Jah*, I am. I was just sitting here telling *Gott* how grateful I am he's provided this wonderful life for us."

"I do that so every day. This past year has been the happiest of my life, you know. I love you, Evie."

"And I love you, too, Benjamin Glick. I love you more with each day that passes."

Benjamin stepped to her and gently put his palms on each side of her face and lowered his head to kiss her lips with a tender sweetness.

Evelyn drank in the taste of him. She remembered once wondering what it would feel like to have his hands touch her. Now she knew.

It was magic.

The End

# Continue Reading...

Thank you for reading **Benjamin's New Beginning.** Are you wondering **what to read next?** Why not read **Trusting Again? Here's a peek for you:**

Dorothy Bontrager couldn't help feeling melancholy as she took down the last of the pine boughs, sprigs of holly, and colorful sparkling ornaments she had used to brighten her *mammi's* house for the holiday just past.

The task of packing away the Christmas decorations had been left to Dorothy, since the older woman had been feeling poorly lately, and Dorothy insisted she go and lie down. Ethel Bontrager had not been in the best of health, even before her husband's passing a few months ago, and it felt as though things had only gotten worse since then. Grief seemed to have sapped the small bit of remaining energy from the older woman, leaving her pale and listless.

When Dorothy's grandfather had suffered a series of small stokes in the weeks leading up to his death, it had fallen mostly to Dorothy to care for him. She had not looked on it as a burden, though, since her grandparents had taken her in after she was orphaned at the age of six.

The older couple had never been much for decorating for the holiday, but Dorothy had tried to make each Christmas with them as cheerful as the Christmases she remembered from before her *mamm* and *daed* passed away.

Most of those memories had grown faded and indistinct over the intervening fourteen years, but she could still recall the feelings of joy, wonder, and hope she'd felt during the special and reverent season with her family before they had been taken from her.

She fingered a golden angel before placing it in the cardboard box where she stored her meager collection of holiday ornaments that had once belonged to her parents. She had struggled more than ever to find her usual Christmas spirit this year. Tucking away the last precious ornament, she closed the cardboard box with a sigh.

Despite her efforts, it had been a solemn holiday for Dorothy and her *mammi*. But she was determined things would be better with the start of the new year in just a few days.

She lifted the box of decorations, intending to take it up to the attic to store it, when she was interrupted by a knock on the front door of the farmhouse. Setting the box back down, she moved to the door to open it.

Her mouth stretched into a wide smile as she saw her friend, Eliza Raber, standing on the front porch. Eliza was bundled up in a coat, scarf, and mittens, her cheeks rosy from the frigid winter air. A gust of icy wind blew through the open door, causing Dorothy to shiver.

### VISIT HERE To Read More!

https://www.ticahousepublishing.com/amish-miller.html

# Thank you for Reading

If you **love Amish Romance**, <u>**Visit Here:**</u>

https://amish.subscribemenow.com/

to find out about all <u>**New Hannah Miller Amish Romance Releases!**</u> **We will let you know as soon as they become available!**

If you enjoyed ***Benjamin's New Beginning,*** would you kindly take a couple minutes to leave a positive review on Amazon? It only takes a moment, and positive reviews truly make a difference. I would be so grateful! Thank you!

**Turn the page to discover more Hannah Miller Amish Romances just for you!**

# More Amish Romance from Hannah Miller

Visit HERE for Hannah Miller's Amish Romance

https://ticahousepublishing.com/amish-miller.html

# About the Author

Hannah Miller has been writing Amish Romance for the past seven years. Long intrigued by the Amish way of life, Hannah has traveled the United States, visiting different Amish communities. She treasures her Amish friends and enjoys visiting with them. Hannah makes her home in Indiana, along with her husband, Robert. Together, they have three children and seven grandchildren. Hannah loves to ride bikes in the sunshine. And if it's warm enough for a picnic, you'll find her under the nearest tree!

Made in United States
North Haven, CT
29 August 2025

72276979R00065